Level 1 is ideal for children who have received some initial reading instruction. Each story is told very simply, using a small number of frequently repeated words.

Special features:

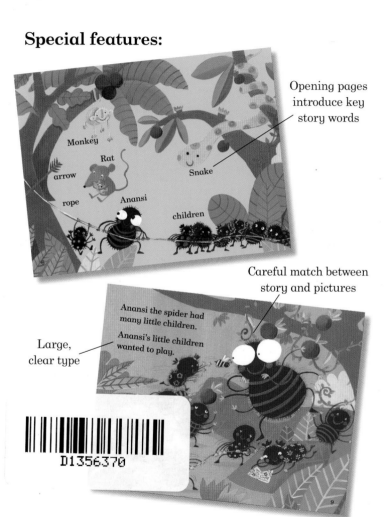

Opening pages introduce key story words

Monkey

Rat

arrow

Snake

rope

Anansi

children

Careful match between story and pictures

Anansi the spider had many little children.

Anansi's little children wanted to play.

Large, clear type

D1356370

Educational Consultant: Geraldine Taylor
Book Banding Consultant: Kate Ruttle

A catalogue record for this book is available from the British Library

Published by Ladybird Books Ltd
80 Strand, London, WC2R 0RL
A Penguin Company

006
© LADYBIRD BOOKS LTD MMXIV
Ladybird, Read It Yourself and the Ladybird Logo are registered or
unregistered trade marks of Ladybird Books Limited.

ISBN: 978-0-72328-048-4

Printed in China

Anansi
Helps a Friend

Written by Lorraine Horsley
Illustrated by Barbara Vagnozzi

Monkey

Rat

arrow

rope

Anansi

6

Snake

children

Anansi the spider had
many little children.

Anansi's little children
wanted to play.

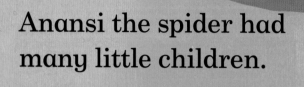

The little spiders went
to see Monkey.

"Can we play with your
children?" they said.

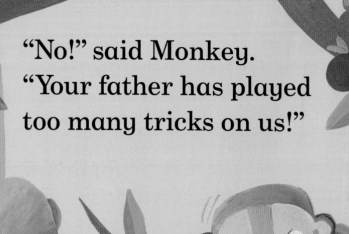

"No!" said Monkey.
"Your father has played
too many tricks on us!"

The little spiders went
to see Rat.

"Can we play with your
children?" they said.

"No!" said Rat.
"Your father has played
too many tricks on us!"

The little spiders
went back to Anansi.

"No one wants to play
with us because of all
your tricks," they said.

One day, Anansi and his children saw Snake with an arrow in his back.

"We must help our
friend," said Anansi.

Anansi and his children
spun a rope around
the arrow.

"Now pull," said Anansi.

They pulled and pulled and pulled... and the arrow came out of Snake's back.

24

25

Rat and Monkey
and all their children
saw Anansi and his little
spiders help Snake.

Anansi and his children
had helped a friend.
Now all the other children
wanted to play with them!

How much do you remember about the story of Anansi Helps a Friend? Answer these questions and find out!

- What do Anansi's children want to do?

- What is stuck in Snake's back?

- What do Anansi and his children do to help Snake?